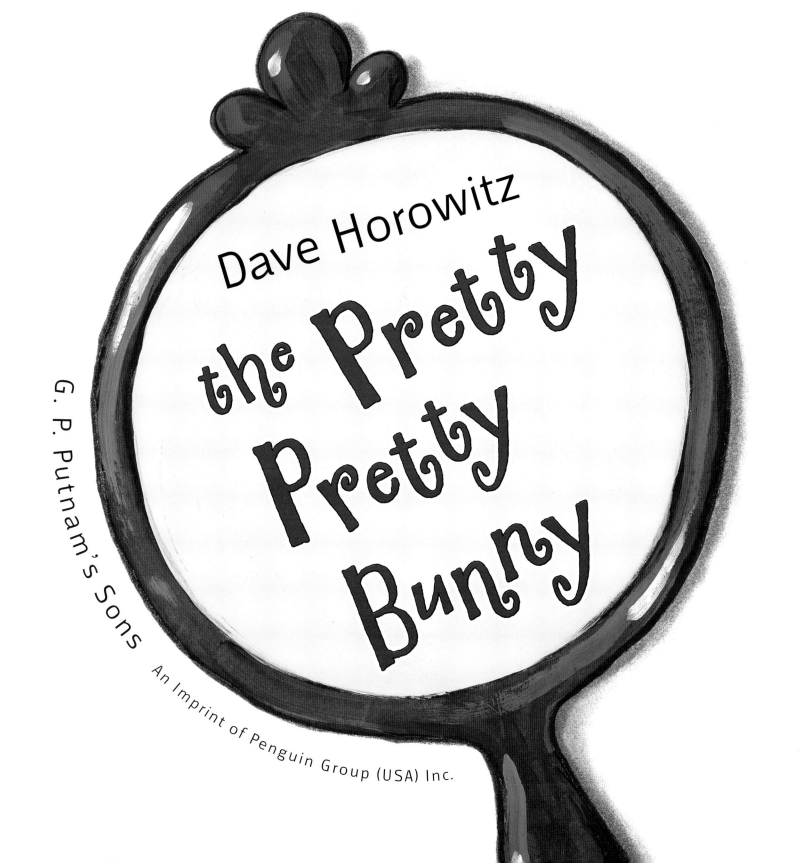

Dave Horowitz

the Pretty Pretty Bunny

G. P. Putnam's Sons   An Imprint of Penguin Group (USA) Inc.

Once upon a time there was a bunny named Narcissa. She was just the prettiest thing in all the land.

Or so she'd say.

One day, Narcissa went for a walk in the woods. There she met a beaver who was hard at work.

"Boy, am I glad I don't look like *that* guy," she said. "Just look at those silly teeth—and what a goofy tail."

A little later, Narcissa met a turtle who was just minding his own business.

"Oh look," she joked, "a bump on a log."

When a moose came by, Narcissa laughed out loud.

"Check out the crazy headgear," she said, pointing rudely.

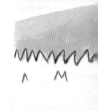

Narcissa stopped when she noticed her reflection in the pond.

"Now, *there,*" she sighed, "is one pretty, pretty bunny."

. . . And that is when the frog emerged.

"CONGRATULATIONS!" said the frog. "I am a magic frog, and I hereby grant you ONE WISH, young bunny."

But Narcissa didn't hear a word of it. She was too busy laughing her head off.

"Wow," she managed between laughs. "Now, *YOU* are one ugly dude!"

This made the magic frog angry.
He shook his fist and placed a
horrible spell upon Narcissa.

and change . . .

And so with each
laugh Narcissa began
to change . . .

and change. Still too pleased with
herself to see what was going on.

Until, that is, she sprouted those antlers. *That* was hard to miss.

When Narcissa got home, she could hardly look at herself.

"Poor me," she cried. "What have I become?"

"I've *become* pretty terrible.

Boy, did I have to be such a BEAST?

"How I *wish* I could do it all

over again."

Well, lucky for Narcissa, she hadn't yet used the magic frog's wish. There was a flash and a bang, and . . .

Once upon a time there was a bunny named Narcissa . . .

*For my mother,
with love.*

ACKNOWLEDGMENTS

The Pretty Pretty Bunny is based very, very loosely on
the Greek myth of Echo and Narcissus (and maybe a little bit
on the American myth of Stephen Colbert).
Thanks to my ever supportive art and editorial team—Nancy Paulsen,
Cecilia Yung, Semadar Megged and Sara Kreger—
for constantly granting me more wishes than I deserve.

G. P. PUTNAM'S SONS

A division of Penguin Young Readers Group.   Published by The Penguin Group.
Penguin Group (USA) Inc., 375 Hudson Street, New York, NY 10014, U.S.A.
Penguin Group (Canada), 90 Eglinton Avenue East, Suite 700, Toronto, Ontario M4P 2Y3, Canada
(a division of Pearson Penguin Canada Inc.).
Penguin Books Ltd, 80 Strand, London WC2R 0RL, England.
Penguin Ireland, 25 St. Stephen's Green, Dublin 2, Ireland (a division of Penguin Books Ltd.).
Penguin Group (Australia), 250 Camberwell Road, Camberwell, Victoria 3124, Australia
(a division of Pearson Australia Group Pty Ltd).
Penguin Books India Pvt Ltd, 11 Community Centre, Panchsheel Park, New Delhi - 110 017, India.
Penguin Group (NZ), 67 Apollo Drive, Rosedale, North Shore 0632, New Zealand (a division of Pearson New Zealand Ltd).
Penguin Books (South Africa) (Pty) Ltd, 24 Sturdee Avenue, Rosebank, Johannesburg 2196, South Africa.
Penguin Books Ltd, Registered Offices: 80 Strand, London WC2R 0RL, England.

Library of Congress Cataloging-in-Publication Data
Horowitz, Dave, 1970–   The pretty pretty bunny / Dave Horowitz.
p. cm.   Summary: A pretty rabbit, Narcissa, makes fun of any creature that is not as lovely as herself until she offends a magic frog and finds her own beauty changing.
[1. Rabbits—Fiction. 2. Pride and vanity—Fiction. 3. Wishes—Fiction. 4. Beauty, Personal—Fiction.] I. Title.   PZ7.H78755Pre 2011   [E]—dc22   2010011571
ISBN 978-0-399-25276-1
1 2 3 4 5 6 7 8 9 10